Kevin the Unicorn

WHY CAN'T WE BE BESTIE-CORNS?

Jessika von Innerebner

Dial Books for Young Readers

To my acquaintances, friends and best friends

Dial Books for Young Readers

An imprint of Penguin Random House LLC, New York

Visit us online at penguinrandomhouse.com

Library of Congress Cataloging-in-Publication Data is available.

Printed in China
ISBN 9781984814807

10 9 8 7 6 5 4 3 2 1

Design by Lily Malcom · Text set in Shag Expert Loung

Everyone knows that EVERYONE loves unicorns.

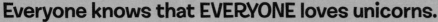

When it comes to making friends,
unicorns really know their stuff.

Do you know who's
SUPER GREAT
at finding new buddies?

Kevin is always ready to give a high five,

lend a helping hoof,

or share a funny joke.

... and the duck just walks away!

HA HA HA

So when a new-corn moved in next door, Kevin couldn't wait to gallop over and say hello.

He just knew they would be friends. No. They would be BEST FRIENDS!

The new-corn was just as excited to meet Kevin.

Hi, I'm Kevin!

Hi, I'm Eric!

Let's be bestie-corns!

To celebrate, Kevin took Eric to his favorite spot in town.

He knew just what to order,
the very best thing on
the menu—of course!

But then . . .

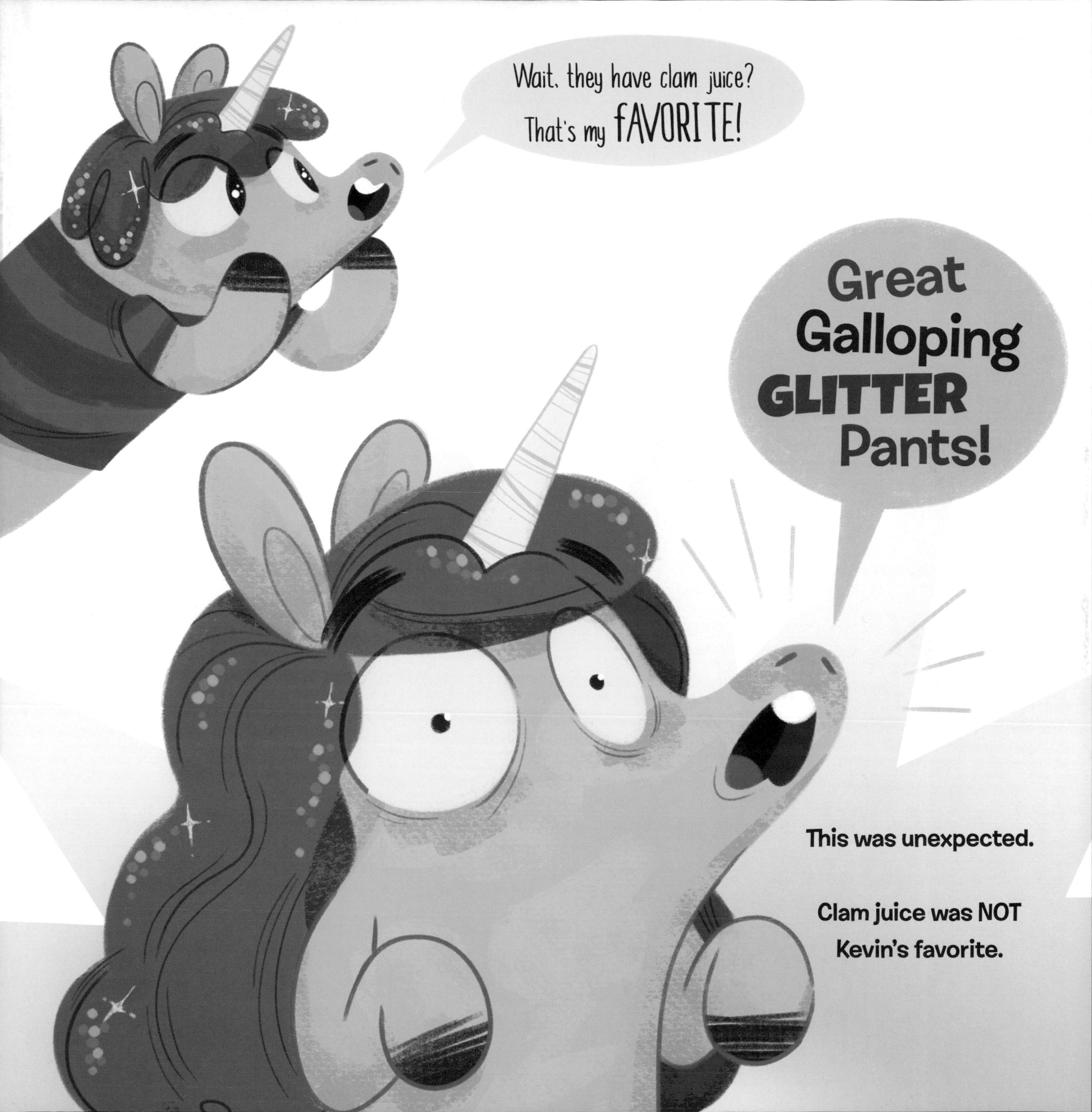

This was unexpected.

Clam juice was NOT Kevin's favorite.

Kevin was determined to make his new friendship work.
So when Eric invited him to a movie night,
he trotted right over.

This is going to be GREAT!
I just know it!

MOVIE NIGHT
POP
CORN

GLITTER SODA

CLAM JUICE

But SCARY movie night was not the do-over Kevin had in mind.

That night, Kevin didn't sleep a wink.
His best friendship with Eric was off to a rocky start,
and he couldn't figure out why!

Eric was up all night too. He knew that if he could just think of the most perfectly perfect activity, he and Kevin would start being BEST best friends.

So Eric suggested they try something outdoorsy.
But Kevin didn't catch the camping bug.

Kevin suggested something sporty.
But Eric couldn't get on board.

They tried something artsy . . .

And something foody . . .

but nothing seemed to work.

Kevin and Eric were flummoxed!
They were supposed to be BESTIE-corns—
but they weren't having
much fun together. At all.

What was going on?

There was only one thing to do.

Oh no! Not more bug bites!

·KEVIN·
YOU'RE INVITED!
TO ERIC'S CAMPING ADVENTURE

And it wasn't going to be easy.

I'm trying to get ramped up, but I just can't.

Eric, you're a very awesome-corn,
I want us to be bestie-corns and do
everything together! But I just
don't like the same things you do!

Thank RAINBOWS!
I totally feel the same way, but
I didn't want to hurtyour feelings.

Instead of trying to force a friendship,
Eric and Kevin decided to just be friendly.

Have a super-duper
camping adventure!

It turns out unicorns aren't
always meant to be bestie-corns . . .

And that's okay.